M000031385

BIG HEART

A Story of a Girl
and Her Horse

By Michael R. Slaughter

Big Heart: A Story of a Girl and Her Horse by Michael Slaughter
Copyright ©2017, 2019. All rights reserved.

ALL RIGHTS RESERVED: No part of this book may be reproduced, stored, or transmitted, in any form, without the express and prior permission in writing of Pen It! Publications. This book may not be circulated in any form of binding or cover other than that in which it is currently published.

This book is licensed for your personal enjoyment only. All rights are reserved. Pen It! Publications does not grant you rights to resell or distribute this book without prior written consent of both Pen It! Publications and the copyright owner of this book. This book must not be copied, transferred, sold or distributed in any way.

Disclaimer: Neither Pen It! Publications, or our authors will be responsible for repercussions to anyone who utilizes the subject of this book for illegal, immoral or unethical use.

This is a work of fiction. The views expressed herein do not necessarily reflect that of the publisher.

This book or part thereof may not be reproduced in any form, stored in a retrieval system, or transmitted in any form by any means-electronic, mechanical, photocopy, recording or otherwise-without prior written consent of the publisher, except as provided by United States of America copyright law.

Keeneland and the Bluegrass Stakes used with permission

Published by Pen It! Publications, LLC
812-371-4128   www.penitpublications.com

ISBN: 978-1-951263-93-5
Cover and Illustrations by Theresa Mangis Sink

Dedicated to
All of my grandchildren

Table of Contents

Chapter One

The enormous crowd cheered wildly as she and her horse thundered down the homestretch of the Kentucky Futurity. A tunnel of sound was all around her and all she could see in front of her was the finish line of the greatest horse race in America. She looked over her shoulder at the horses racing behind her. They seemed far away. There was no doubt in her mind that she was going to be the winning jockey of this Kentucky Futurity - and only 18 years old at that!

She heard her name being shouted from the stands, "Andy," short for Andrea. What a day, she thought.

But then the unthinkable happened. Almost without warning, her horse began to slow down. Slower and slower as the horses behind her began to get closer and closer. This couldn't be happening. She was being passed by all of the other horses. Yet, the crowd continued to call her name.

"Andy. Andy - wake up," her mother was saying.

She rubbed the sleep from her eyes. She had been dreaming that same dream again – she was always about to win the Kentucky Futurity, yet always lost at the very end.

Her mother said, "Andy, it's time. Misty Dawn is having her foal."

Here in the middle of a very cold and dark night, the family's thoroughbred mare was having her newborn son. Andy's father was already in the cold, drafty barn when Mary and Andy got inside. There in the straw was a very small, very weak looking colt. Misty Dawn nuzzled her son's head.

It was unseasonably cold on the night he was born. The wind made a whistling noise though the big cracks in the sides of the old barn. The air inside the dark and drafty barn was as cold as the air outside.

But Misty Dawn was used to the cold and dark. She was used to the hard life of living on a poor horse farm in Kentucky.

The rich horse farms had very nice barns for their special thoroughbred horses. The air in those barns was warmed by heaters. The lights glowed with a bright yellow for each stall. The hay was changed and fluffed every day to make the stalls more comfortable for the horses. Those horses were fed oats, corn, barley and bran with vitamins and other special things to help the horses to grow bigger, stronger, and faster.

On those rich horse farms, when it came a mare's time to have her baby, she was moved to an extra special barn just for her and her new foal. Someone stayed with the mare to make sure everything went well and that there were no problems with the birth. She always had cool, clean water to drink, and a nice soft blanket to keep her warm. For those horses, life was easy and good.

Misty Dawn's life had not been easy. She didn't have a heated barn to stay in. Her stall was only lit with a lantern. There was no one there to watch over her to help her if there were problems with the birth of her son. If Misty Dawn wanted her hay fluffed up, she did it herself with her nose. At times, there was no cool fresh water to help her dry throat and no warm blanket to protect her against the cold night air.

Misty Dawn, and her son, lived at a farm called Richland Stables. Yet, Richland Stables was far from rich. The owners of the farm, Mary and John Bell, were poor farmers just trying to make a living by doing some farming. Mary and John had only owned one thoroughbred, Misty Dawn.

Misty Dawn was the hope for the farm and the Bells. She hadn't been able to race for years. Even when she was racing, she had not won a single race. Now she was too old to race. However, now, with her son, there was hope again at Richland Stables.

Some time back, the Bells were facing many problems. They had bills to pay and no money. They even had taken out loans to pay for feed for Misty Dawn and to repair their old truck. They could not pay the taxes that were coming due on their farm. At that point they had begun to look to Misty Dawn as their only hope.

The plan began to develop this way. Mary and John had a daughter named Andrea. Everyone called her Andy. Andy had two things that she wanted to do in her life - she wanted to ride racehorses and she wanted to go to college.

Andy worked as an exercise rider at Keeneland Racetrack, which was very close to her farm. She would save the money she made to help pay for college after she graduated from high school. Every morning, Andy would get up at four o'clock so that she could be at the track before dawn. Then she would ride the horses as a way for training them to race. At eight o'clock she would run out to the highway in time to catch her bus for high school.

One day her mom and dad came to her and said, "Andy, we know that you have worked hard to save your money for college. We have never asked you to do anything except work hard in school and save your money. But now we have a big problem."

"What is it?" Andy asked.

"You know, Andy," her dad began, this farm faces many, many bills. We've had two bad growing seasons in a row."

"Yes, I know," said Andy.

"Well," her dad continued, "we just can't keep on going. We have got to get some big money and your mother, and I have been thinking about Misty Dawn."

"You're not going to sell her - are you Dad?" Andy said anxiously. "I know she's not the best thoroughbred in Kentucky, but she is my friend and I couldn't stand to lose her."

"We know that, Andy. We don't want to have to sell her either. So, we have been thinking of something else for her. What if we matched her up with a really good racehorse? Maybe then she would have a colt that we could sell at the yearling sales," her dad said.

Andy's eyes got happier. "Yeah, that would be great. We could make enough money off of that one sale to pay all of our bills."

"But, Andy, that takes money to make a match like that. An owner of a really good sire would ask a lot of money for a match." Hesitantly, her dad said, "so, we were wondering if we could use your college fund money to pay for that match with a good thoroughbred sire."

Andy didn't think for even a second. "Sure, Dad, anything to save our farm."

And that is what happened. Andy's savings were not enough to buy the services of the best racing champion. So, Richland Stables had to settle for another horse- one that had only raced a few times but had won two of his races. The horse was named Red Rider. In Red Rider, Mary, John and Andy hoped that his bloodlines were good enough to help Misty

Dawn to produce a fine colt that would be strong and healthy.

Misty Dawn also knew how important she and her baby would be for the farm. If her colt could be sold for two hundred thousand dollars or more, everything would be fine. She knew that some yearlings in the past had sold for a million dollars or more. That may be too much for her to hope for with a father like Red Rider and a mother like her, she thought.

Then the time came for the birth of her son. Misty Dawn looked down at her new son. Then she looked up at Mary and John and Andy. She had hoped to see happiness on their faces. But all that she saw in the dim lantern light was sadness. Misty Dawn looked back down at her new son. He was thin and weak, and so small. He looked sick. He did not look healthy like she had wanted him to be. In fact, Misty Dawn was afraid that her son would not be strong enough to live through the cold, long night. She nuzzled him and cleaned him off. She pushed the hay closer to him. Then she lay down beside him so that his shaking little body could feel her warmth.

Mary, John, and Andy, their heads bowed, their arms around each other, took the lantern and walked slowly out of the barn. Misty Dawn was now alone with her son in the darkness. Only the light from the stars cast a little light into the stall. Just the two of them were together in the cold and the dark. She tried to tell her new son that she loved him. She tried to tell him that he was beautiful to her. He weakly nuzzled his head closer to her neck. In the cold and the dark, Misty Dawn watched as her son went to sleep in the hay.

Chapter Two

The next morning the air was still crisp. But with the sun beaming down, the air in the barn began to slowly warm up. Misty Dawn was still watching as her son awakened to a fresh new day. The first full day of his life. A sweet smell of warm hay up in the loft above them drifted down and into their noses.

Soon, Andy rushed into the barn. She gave Misty Dawn fresh oats and poured her son fresh new water from the well. As Misty Dawn ate and drank, her new son nursed her milk.

Andy was happy. She said to Misty Dawn, "Well, Misty, you did it! Your new son looks great! I know he is going to be a fast racehorse." Andy patted Misty Dawn on her nose as she spoke quietly to her. "I know he doesn't look very big or strong. And I know that Mom and Dad are a little disappointed in him. But, Misty, you know about racing. And I know about racing. We can help him to be his best. While he is young, you must teach him how to run through the meadow. Show him how he can use his short legs to run like the wind through the bluegrass."

Now Andy patted the side of the little colt. "We can't give you a name, little one. When you are sold in the fall, your new owners will give you an official name. Until then we will just call you - 'Little One." You may be little and weak now, but with your mother's help and mine, people will soon be calling you 'Fast One'."

Looking back to Misty Dawn, Andy said, "Well, Misty, I have got to catch the school bus. I'll be back this afternoon to see how you are doing."

In a moment, Andy was gone. Misty Dawn turned her head to see her nursing son. "Little One," she thought. She had hoped that he would be called "Big One" or "Strong One" not "Little One." But, no matter, he was her son and she loved him for what he was.

Misty Dawn thought about what Andy had said. She would help her son to become fast. She was amazed at how differently he looked in the daylight. In the night he had looked like he might not live. Now, he looked much better. Misty Dawn thought, "My son has just fought his first battle. He had to fight through the night to stay alive. He fought death and he won. I am so proud of my new son! Andy may call you "Little One," but I will call you "Big Heart" because that is really what you are."

Misty Dawn turned all of the way around as her son finished nursing. She looked straight into his eyes. She had to try to tell him what she thought. He looked up at his mother. She thought, "My son, I am very proud of you."

The little foal looked deeply into his mother's eyes. He was understanding what she was thinking.

Misty Dawn thought, "You have fought a hard battle and you have won. John and Mary do not know you like I do. Even Andy doesn't know you like I do. You have a big heart and you will never quit trying to be the best you can be. That is very important for a racehorse. You must never give up. You must always do your best. There will be days when you will be racing against bigger and stronger horses. But none of those horses will have won the kind of battle you have already won. None of them will have raced the kind of race you have already raced. Last night you raced with Death and you won."

This was Misty Dawn's first lesson to her new son. A thoroughbred can never give up until the race is over. Win or not --a thoroughbred must always do his best.

Chapter Three

The days grew gradually longer and warmer. Winter slowly changed to Spring. As March ended and April began, the sad little farm took on a fresh new feeling. Spring on a farm is always like a new beginning. The brown scrub grass in the fields turned to a bright green. From a hilltop overlooking the big meadow of Richland Stables, the special grass of Kentucky sometimes looked a little blue in the early morning light. That was why some people called that grass in that part of the country "bluegrass."

The meadow looked like a pretty picture. Small purple flowers and bright yellow dandelions dotted the green grass and added even more sparkle to the color of the bluegrass. Running though the meadow at Richland Stables was a small stream of fresh, clean water. The stream began as a small spring with water bubbling up out of the ground. On its way to the surface, the water passed though the limestone rock that was underground. The limestone gave the water part of its minerals as the water passed through it. Many people believed that it was this special limestone water and the special bluegrass that grows from that water that make the bones of the Kentucky thoroughbred horses so strong.

Misty Dawn led her young son into the meadow. Now, from the hilltop the picture was even prettier. In the flat green meadow, surrounded by a double row of black fencing, were two beautiful thoroughbred horses drinking from the sparkling brook. One of the horses was large and strong. The other horse was small and weak.

All over the farm, a new season was beginning. Mary and John faced more and more bills. They had to do something, or they would lose the farm even before they had a chance to sell the colt at the fall yearling sales. They had an idea. In Louisville, a company that made and sold pickles was looking for farmers to grow cucumbers. John went to the factory. A man at the factory gave John some special cucumber seeds and some fertilizer. John and Mary planned on growing the cucumbers for the pickle factory. The work would be hard and hot.

They would have to pick cucumbers every single day. Only small cucumbers were used to make pickles. They would have to pick the cucumbers when they were small because once they got too big, they would not be able to sell them to the factory. Every day they would have to take their cucumbers to the weighing station in their old truck. They would be paid according to how much the small cucumbers weighed. By growing and selling cucumbers, John and Mary hoped to be able to keep up on their bills.

With the warmer weather, Andy was back at Keeneland Race Track every morning. She still had her job as an exercise rider. Instead of saving her money for college, now her money went to buy feed for the two horses at Richland Stables. Andy knew that if the new colt could be sold at the yearling sales, there would be a lot of money; money to pay off the farm taxes and any of the bills, and money to pay for her college tuition starting in January.

In the meadow, Misty Dawn watched with pride as her young son playfully chased after a butterfly. His steps were not very graceful. He did not yet know how to move with power and smoothness. He did not yet know how to run like a thoroughbred racehorse.

Misty Dawn came up to him and stood by the fence, watching as the butterfly flitted away. She touched his back with her nose. Then she turned and slowly ran away from him. He turned and started to run after her. Even though she was not running fast, he could not catch up to her. His short little legs could not move fast enough. She ran slowly all the way to the other end of the meadow. He chased her all of the way. When she stopped, he caught up to her. Then she turned and ran slowly back to the other end of the meadow. Again, he ran after her. She did this many, many times that day. Between runs they would go to the cool, clear brook and drink the water.

While resting by the stream, Misty Dawn looked into her son's eyes. She thought, "My son, you must always run as fast as you can. Another thing that is important to a racehorse is to be able to run long distances. When the time comes when you begin to think that you can't run any more, your courage must take over. It will be your Big Heart that will keep you running fast even beyond what you think is possible."

He looked into her eyes. He knew that his mother was telling him important things that he had to remember.

Misty Dawn thought, "Son, a day will come when you will need your courage. On that day, all of the horses racing against you will be fast. Maybe all of them will be bigger than you and all of them will be able to run a long distance. But I know that you will be able to win that race because of your Big Heart. You have more courage than any other horse I have ever known. Your Big Heart will let you forget about the hurting in your lungs and the growing weakness in your legs. Your Big Heart will keep you running while the other horses will be tiring and quitting. Sometimes it is not the fastest horse that wins the race. Sometimes it is the horse with the biggest heart, the one with the most courage. And, my son, that horse will be you."

Her son listened and understood. He would make his mother proud. He would never quit.

Each day throughout the Spring, Misty Dawn ran up and back in the meadow while her son would chase her. Each day, she went a little faster. Each day, she ran a little farther. Each day, little by little, she watched as her son became stronger and stronger, and faster and faster. He was learning how to run like a thoroughbred. He was learning how to run smoothly.

As the Spring turned into the very hot days of summer, Misty Dawn started the next part of her plan. She stopped running up and back in the meadow. That was not how horses ran in a race.

Now, she started running around the edge of the large meadow. That was how horses ran on a racetrack - in a large oval. She had to teach her son to run fast while turning as well as when running straight.

Around and around the meadow the two horses ran. Whenever they stopped at the stream to rest and drink the cool water, Misty Dawn would tell her son important things about being a thoroughbred racehorse. He listened and he remembered.

As August turned to September, the races around the edge of the meadow became faster and faster. In her mind, Misty Dawn dreamed that the meadow was a large racetrack. The track in her mind was filled with big crowds of people. The people cheered and yelled as she and her son raced. The bands played happy music. The flags snapped in the wind. It was time for the big test.

Misty Dawn started around the meadow as fast as she could run. Her son raced by her side. Stride for stride they ran together. She could not run any faster. Around one turn in the meadow, and her son stayed right with her. Down the side of the meadow and still her son raced with her. The wind in her ears sounded like the roar of a large crowd cheering them on. Her feet pounded into the ground. Her blood pounded in her brain. Yet still her son ran beside her.

On the other side of the meadow they ran, stride for stride. Misty Dawn didn't know if she could keep going at that fast pace. She had never run this fast for this long before. But she knew that she had to keep going. Her lungs had trouble breathing, her eyes had trouble seeing, and her legs had trouble running. Still she ran as fast as she could, and her son ran beside her. They had already run more than a mile.

Misty Dawn's lungs felt as though they were going to burst. But then she watched as her son began to run even faster. He would show his mother how he could run. He would show her that he would not quit. He raced ahead of her to the finish. He was running faster at the end of their race than he had been running at the beginning.

That day he ran through the meadow like the wind in the bluegrass. He ran so fast that he felt as though he feet were not even touching the ground. It felt like he was flying instead of running. It felt wonderful! He knew that he was going to be a good racehorse. He was going to be a racehorse that would make his mother proud.

Misty Dawn watched him drink slowly at the cool brook. She felt very proud of her fast, strong son. She knew that as the days were growing shorter, her son would be leaving her. When the day of the sale came, she would no longer see her son. He would be gone from her life forever.

Chapter Four

Fall was a special time on a Kentucky horse farm. The mornings were crisp with the chilly air. There was smell in the wind of wood stoves burning in the mornings. Everywhere in this country the trees took on a new beauty. The dark green colors of the leaves of summer had changed to the many colors of fall. Now the trees had leaves that were fire engine red, or fire hydrant orange, or sunset yellow. Bright colors were everywhere. The grass was coated with a thin glistening coat of white frost in the early morning stillness.

Fall was a season of endings and beginnings for Richland Stables. For John and Mary, it was the end of a long cucumber growing season. It was a time to look back with happiness at the money that they had made. Fall was also the beginning of the winter season. There was wood to cut to heat the house during the cold winter months ahead. There was corn to pick and store to help feed the horses.

For Andy, fall was an ending and a beginning. The summer was over. Her high school life was over. For her, the summer had been filled with work on the farm. She now spent her daytimes helping her dad around the farm and her mother in the kitchen canning fruits and vegetables. Andy was becoming a young woman. Each morning before dawn, she would go the racetrack to exercise horses. During the day she would help her father and mother. In the evenings she would go back to the track to help with the horses in the growing darkness.

For the son of Misty Dawn, Fall was also an ending and a beginning. The free romps in the meadow were over. Andy was working with him every day to look his best. His legs were carefully wrapped with cloth to protect them. Andy did not want to take any chances that he would have scars or scratches on his legs when it came time for the sale. Good looking legs were very important to a thoroughbred. Every day Andy brushed and groomed his reddish-brown coat.

During the summer he had filled out. He was healthy looking, and he was beginning to look like a real racehorse. Even though he was shorter than other thoroughbreds his age, he still looked great.

For Misty Dawn the Fall was an ending and a beginning as well. It was the end of her fun-filled times in the meadow with her son. Now, when they went to the meadow, Andy was always there with them. Her son was no longer free to chase butterflies. He was now too valuable to take a chance on hurting an ankle or hoof. Fall was the beginning of the end of Misty Dawn's time with her son. Soon he would be sold, and she would never see him again. Misty Dawn did not know what to think. She was confused. She wanted her son to be a successful racehorse. She wanted him to be sold for a lot of money to help the farm, but she wanted to be with him. She missed those days in the meadow when they stood together at the brook. She felt sad that those days were soon to be over forever.

A week before the yearling sale, John went to the sales office at Keeneland. He wanted to enter Misty Dawn's son in the sale. John had never tried to sell a horse at the sale before. As he opened the door to the sales office, a secretary looked up. "Yes, sir," she said, "can I help you?"

"Yes," John said, "I am John Bell of Richland Stables." He paused because he didn't really know what to say next.

"Richland Stables?" the secretary repeated. This was a new name to her. She had never heard of a horse farm by that name.

"Yes," John started again, "it is a small horse farm near here."

"Oh," the secretary said as she looked back down at her paperwork. She thought to herself, "Why is this man bothering me now - just a week before the yearling sales?"

John announced, "We want to have a colt sold in the yearling sales next week."

The secretary jumped up from her desk. "Next week!" She couldn't believe what she was hearing. "Didn't you know that all of the entries for that sale have been in this office for over a month?"

John apologized. "This is the first colt we have ever tried to sell at the yearling sales. We just didn't know." He went on, "but we have to sell this colt. The future of our farm depends upon it."

The secretary was not happy. "Well, I'm not sure I can get this worked out. The auction booklet is already at the printers."

"I understand. We sure would appreciate anything you can do for us," John said.

"You are only selling one horse?" she asked.

John nodded his head.

"Some of our farms have thirty or forty horses to sell at this sale. Most have at least ten horses to sell. No one has only one horse."

But John pleaded again, "We have to sell this colt at the sale. Our whole future depends upon it."

"I'll do what I can," she said. "Here, fill out this entry form." She added, "And hurry up. I have a million things to do and little time in which to do them."

After a few minutes, John was back at the secretary's desk with the completed entry form.

She looked up again at John. "That will be two hundred dollars, and remember, no matter what happens you won't get any of that money back."

John gave her a check for the fee. The secretary took his money and then looked through a tall stack of papers. She then handed him a small piece of paper. She said, "Your colt will be number 472, the last horse to be sold on the last day of the sale. That is the best I can do."

John thanked her for her help and started to turn away and head for the door.

However, the secretary was not done talking. "Your colt may not be listed in the auction booklet because it is so late. And there are no stall locations left for your colt. They have all been taken by the other owners who got here before you. You are going to have to take what you can get. I am sorry but next time, get here sooner."

Again, John apologized and thanked her for her help. He walked out of the office with the valuable piece of paper in his hand. Attached to the paper was a sticker with the number "472" written on it in big numbers. The sticker was to be put on the hip of Richland Stables only colt in the yearling sales. From that point until he was sold, Misty Dawn's son would be known as "Hip number 472."

Chapter Five

The yearling sale was a Fall festival in horse country. All of the large horse farms in Kentucky were there. The largest farms rented whole barns filled with twenty or more stalls. These barns were decorated with bright awnings and flags with the names of the farms on them. The barns did not look like regular horse barns. The looked more like a Sultan's tent filled with the finest young horses that money could buy. Each stall cost three hundred dollars.

Some of the stalls were not used for the horses at all. Some of the stalls were set up like bedrooms for the groomers and handlers for the horses. These stalls had cloth all around them. They had a curtain for a door. Inside the stalls were chairs, beds, tables and lamps. Each stall floor was covered with sweet-smelling cedar wood chips.

Outside of each stall was a brightly colored metal trunk. The colors on the trunks were the same as the flags and awnings. On each trunk was the name of the farm or stable painted on it in fancy letters. Inside the trunks were bridles, combs, and brushes. Everything was in the trunk to help make the horse look as great as it could look.

Each of those horses was treated in a very special way. Every morning, they were given baths with sweet smelling shampoo. Their manes and tails were combed to look silky smooth. Their coats were brushed to make them shiny and thick.

The first day of the yearling sales was a "preview day." No horses were sold on that day. That day was just so the potential buyers could look at each horse up close.

Very rich horse buyers from all over the world came to the yearling sales. They walked among the brightly decorated barns. The buyers always went to the royal blue barn of Rolling Hills Farm. Rolling Hills Farm was famous all over the world for having the finest horses for sale. That farm had great sires and mares which produced horses that became winners on the racetracks around the country and even the world. All of the horse buyers knew that Rolling Hills horses had won more Kentucky Races that any other stable. Because of that, everyone knew that they would have the best yearlings at the sale. Rolling Hills Farm had the honor of the first thirty horses in the sale.

The next barn beside Rolling Hills was the bright red and gold colors of Forest Creek Stables. All of the buyers were also excited about the forty horses that Forest Creek had in the sale. No one was really sure which of these two horse farms would have the honor of selling the most expensive horse at the sale. However, everyone was sure one of them would have that honor.

The rich horse buyers moved slowly through each of the brightly colored barns. At each stall, the buyers would stop and talk to the farm owners and trainers. The buyers were given fancy wines to drink and special sandwiches to eat. While drinking and eating they would talk quietly to the trainers about each colt in their barn. They would look at the colt's hip number and look him up in the auction booklet.

A yearling auction listing had a pretty picture of the colt, or filly, if the horse were a female. Below the picture was a listing of the yearling's father and mother. After that, the yearling's grandfathers and grandmothers were listed. Families were very important in horse racing. The bloodlines of the grandfather to the father and from the father to the son or daughter were very important. Rich horse owners believed that if the grandfather and father were fast, the son or daughter would be fast as well. Grandmothers and mothers were just as important in the bloodlines of a racehorse.

Each of the brightly colored barns was busy with parties being held for the buyers. One barn was not brightly decorated. That barn was not close to the other barns. There were no parties at that barn. It was the barn for the farms that only had one, two, or three horses in the sale. It was the barn that housed the small farms' horses. It was the barn where Richland Stables horse was housed.

Richland Stables could not afford an extra three hundred dollars for Andy. Andy slept on an old army cot in the same stall as her colt. There was no curtain for the door. There were no chairs and tables and lamps. There was just the cot and Andy and her horse with a bare light bulb hanging over their heads.

No one came to see Richland Stables' only colt. His hip number and picture did not get into the auction booklet. No one knew he was even there except for John, and Mary, and Andy. Of course, Misty Dawn knew that he was there. And she knew that she would never see him again.

Chapter Six

The next day was filled with excitement and anticipation as the actual sale began. Rolling Hills Farm was very happy with its yearlings. Each horse sold for at least one million dollars. The sale went just as well for Forrest Creek Stables. In fact, all of the farm owners were happy on that first day. The sales were generally very high. All of the buyers were also very happy. This had been a very good start to the yearling sales.

That evening there was a big party in a giant tent set up near Rolling Hills Farm's barn. The band played loud, happy dance music. Very good wine and very good food was served to everyone. The horse farm owners and the horse buyers were all at the big party. Everyone had a very good time.

In the dark barn away from the party, Andy and her colt tried to sleep. They had to look their best when it became their turn to come into the sales ring. It was hard sleeping with all of the music, laughter, and noise. Finally, at 2:30 in the morning, the party stopped. Finally, the music and the noise ended. Finally, Andy and her colt could sleep.

This same scene was repeated each night after each day's sale. Each night the air was filled with loud music and loud talking and laughter. Each night the farm owners were happy. And each night the horse buyers were happy. Each night, Andy and her colt had trouble going to sleep.

Finally, the last day of the sale arrived. It would now be Richland Stables' turn to be happy and party all night. Andy got up early on this last day of the sale. She gave her colt a nice warm bath. She spent extra time washing and drying him. Everything had to be perfect. She combed the young colt's mane and tail. She carefully brushed his chestnut colored coat. She polished his hooves. Everything had to look perfect, and it did. Except for being a little shorter and smaller than all of the other horses in the sale, her colt was as great looking as any of the others.

Andy was satisfied that her colt looked his best. Now she had to work on herself to look her best too. She had to look like she was part of a rich horse farm. She went home and took a bath and then put on her best riding suit. It was the only riding suit she had. But she knew that she looked good in it. She and her colt looked very good.

John and Mary also put on their very best clothes. The ones they wore to church every Sunday. All three of them squeezed into the old farm truck and headed back to Keeneland for the sale of their horse.

Andy was ready to lead her colt into the sales arena. However, there was one last thing to do. She took the special sticker from her pocket. It had adhesive on the back so that it would hold temporarily on the horse's skin. It was her colt's sticker, number 472. It was their entry into the sales ring. She carefully placed it on the hip of her horse.

Hip number 472 was ready. Andy was ready. She knew her parents were already inside the arena awaiting the big moment.

Time dragged on. The hours slipped away. It grew later, and later in the afternoon. Andy thought, "When will they call us?" The sun began to dip lower in the Autumn sky and then to drop below the tree line.

Finally, the call they had been waiting for came. "Hip number 472 to the sales ring, please." Andy's heart raced as she led her beautiful looking thoroughbred toward the sales arena. Then, finally they were inside the ring.

Andy looked around and up into the stands. She saw her mother and father. The stands should have been filled with owners and buyers. But most of the seats were empty. Most of the buyers had left already. There were no other owners in the stands because Richland Stables had the very last horse for sale at the yearling sales. It seemed that most of the buyers had already purchased all of the horses they wanted to buy. Now, all they wanted was to get to that night's party.

The arena was very quiet as the auctioneer announced, "And now, Ladies and Gentlemen, Richland Stables presents Hip number 472, by Red Rider and out of Misty Dawn." His words echoed in the big arena.

In the center of the ring, Misty Dawn's son stood as straight and as tall as he could. He would make his mother proud of him. He would make Andy proud of him. His eyes were bright, and his ears stood up proudly.

Andy was ready for the bidding to begin.

The auctioneer continued, " Hip number 472 from Richland Stables was a late entry and is not listed in your booklet. Now what am I bid for this beautiful chestnut colt? Let's start the bidding at two hundred thousand dollars!"

Andy's heart felt like it had jumped up into her throat. John and Mary nervously held hands so tightly that their hands started to hurt. Andy's ears strained to hear the opening yells from the bid spotters which would indicate that the buyers were bidding on her horse. She could hear no yells.

The auctioneer said, "Come on, Ladies and Gentlemen, what am I bid for Hip number 472 out of Misty Dawn? Will you start the bidding at one hundred thousand dollars?"

Still, Andy could hear no yells. There were no bids.

"Please, Ladies and Gentlemen, this is the last horse of the sale. Let's start the bidding, please." The auctioneer pleaded. "Do I hear an offer? Fifty thousand dollars? Do I hear fifty?"

The auctioneer was growing desperate, 'How about twenty-five thousand?" Still there were no bids. "Ten thousand? How about ten?" he said.

Andy and her colt stood in the center of the ring in the middle of an arena, which was almost completely empty. The Auctioneer's words bounced off of the walls in the back of the hall and echoed back down upon them. While the Auctioneer continued to lower the bid in an effort to get someone - anyone - to bid on the horse, Andy became more and more embarrassed for the proud colt that stood beside her.

Finally, Andy turned and looked up at the auctioneer. Andy yelled, so that he would be able to hear her, "Excuse me, Sir. Richland Stables withdraws Hip number 472 from the sale. Thank You."

With their heads held up proudly, Andy and her yearling walked out of the sales ring. The auctioneer brought down his gavel with a loud "bang," The yearling sales were over.

Chapter Seven

John and Mary Bell slowly got up into the old truck. They had to go back into the barn area to pick up Andy and their yearling. Sadness was in John's eyes; tears were in Mary's. Both John and Mary felt like all was lost. They would not be able to hold out much longer. Their farm would have to be sold in order to pay their bills. Without some hope for the future, the tax collectors could make them sell their home and their farm.

Without the money from the sale of the colt, the hope for the future was gone. All during the spring and summer, the hope for this sale had kept everyone on the farm going. The hope for the sale had given Andy, Mary, and John the strength to keep going.

That hope had given Andy the strength to get up before dawn and go to bed long after dark while working hard each day. That hope had given Mary and John the strength to do the back-breaking cucumber farming just to get a few extra dollars a day. That hope had given John the courage to tell his creditors to wait just a little bit longer.

Now that hope was gone. Without that hope, all of the strength and courage was gone. John was tired. He was so tired that he could barely drive the truck. Mary was tired. She was so tired that she could barely hold up her head. Back at the barn with her horse, Andy was tired. She sat heavily on the edge of her old army cot. She held her head in her hands.

Everyone was worn out. Everyone was so very tired. They were tired in their bodies. But more importantly, they were tired in their minds. The hope that had been in their minds, had given their bodies the strength and courage to keep going. Now, that hope was gone. The energy was gone. The strength was gone.

Everyone was tired. Everyone, that is except their colt - hip number 472. He was not tired. But he was confused, and he was mad. Why didn't any of the buyers want him? He looked good. He ran fast. He did not give up. A smart horse buyer should have known that he could do those things. They should have been able to see it in his eyes. It confused him that the buyers did not know these things about him. It made him mad that they did not like him.

Misty Dawn had told him that he must never quit. As he looked around, he saw that Andy was acting like she had quit. That confused him even more. Was it all right for people to quit but not for horses to quit? He did not know the answer.

But he was sure of some things. He was sure that he would never give up and that he would always keep trying to be the best he could be. He was also sure that someday everyone would know that he was a good racehorse. The buyers may not have known about him on this day, but some day everyone would know about him. He would show everyone.

He knew that he had to start by showing Andy. Andy had given up. He could not let Andy give up on him. He knew that he was the future for Richland Stables. Because he had not been sold, there was no money now, but some day he could race, and he could win. Someday there would be money in his future and in the future of Richland Stables.

He looked over to Andy. She was still sitting with her head in her hands. He nuzzled Andy's hands with his nose. Andy did not move. She continued to sit on the edge of the cot with her head in her hands. He pushed her hand with his nose again. Slowly, Andy looked up, and when she did, she looked straight up and into his eyes. "What could this colt want?" she thought.

Slowly, very slowly, an idea began to form in Andy's mind. And she began to think to herself, "Can I do it? Can he do it? Can we do it?"

The colt knew exactly what she was thinking. He bobbed his head up and down. "Yes, we can," he thought.

Andy remembered watching this little horse run with Misty Dawn in the big meadow. She immediately began to feel better. She thought to herself, "Yes, he can do it. I have got to help him do it. We will do it together!"

Even so, she could still think of problems. Time was a problem, money was a problem, and her parents were a problem. Somehow, they all had to overcome those problems. She would start with her parents first.

Soon, they were riding back to the farm with the colt in the back of the old truck. While they were riding, Andy began to tell her parents about her idea. She said, "You both know that we have a fast horse in the back of this truck."

John replied, "It is a shame for us that the we are the only people that know he is fast. The buyers sure didn't realize it."

"That may all be true," Andy said, but John interrupted her. "We needed that money from the sale," he said.

"Yes, I know," Andy said, "but if we could hold out just a little longer, we can race him ourselves. We can race him as a two-year-old next Spring."

Her dad said, "I just don't know if we can hold out that long. Everybody wants their money now."

Andy replied, "We have GOT to hold out that long. He can win. I know he can win."

"Who is going to train him?" John asked. "We don't have the money to pay for a horse trainer."

"I am going to train him, Dad" Andy said. "I have been around the racetrack for years as an exercise rider. I have watched the trainers with their horses. I know what to do and how to do it."

At that point, John and Mary began to dream the same dream that Andy had been dreaming. John said, "Do you really think that you can train him to be a winner?"

"I think he is already a winner, Dad. All I have to do is to show him how to not be a loser," Andy said.

Mary joined in, "We have got to give him a name. It has to be a good, strong name. His name must be just like him."

Andy thought for a second, then said, "I think I have a good name for him. How about 'Red Dawn'?"

"'Red Dawn,'" Andy's mother repeated, "I like that. Red Dawn means a start to a bright new day. That is what he is for us and our farm, the start of a bright new day."

Now everyone in the truck was sharing the same dream for the future. It was John and Mary's dream. It was Andy's dream. Most importantly, it was Red Dawn's dream.

It was a dream and hope for the future. It was a dream that HAD to come true.

Chapter Eight

John and Mary mailed the application to the Jockey Club in New York and registered Misty Dawn's son as "Red Dawn." There were many rules to be followed in giving a horse a name. One of the most important rules was that the name could not have been used before. Red Dawn was a good name to use. The registration papers were filled out and a number was given to the colt.

It was a number that only Red Dawn would have. It would be his number forever. His number was tattooed on the inside of his upper lip.

Red Dawn was a good name because his mother was Misty Dawn and his father was Red Rider. He would carry both of his parent's name with him as he raced. He was very happy and proud about that.

Andy started to work with Red Dawn the very next day. After exercising horses in the early mornings at Keeneland, Andy would come home to be with Red Dawn. There were many things that Andy would have to teach him.

The more she worked with Red Dawn, the more she loved him and understood him. Red Dawn was a good name. However, it was not a friendly name.

Andy was a good friend of Red Dawn. She started calling him "Little Red" as a nickname. It was a friendly name that Andy loved.

Many years ago, there had been a famous chestnut thoroughbred named Man-O-War. Most people thought he was the best racehorse that ever lived. Compared to most racehorses he was bigger and taller than the rest. Everyone called him "Big Red."

Red Dawn was a chestnut color like Man-O-War, but he was not bigger and taller than all of the other horses. In fact, he was quite a bit smaller and shorter than the other horses. "Little Red" was a good name for him.

Andy slowly let Little Red get used to the racing bridle that he would have to wear when he was racing. Little Red had never seen a racing bridle before. He had never had a bit in his mouth. He had never had a saddle on his back. Andy showed Little Red what these things were by putting them on Misty Dawn first. Little Red saw that these things did not hurt his mother. So, he was sure that they would not hurt him either. Andy talked to Little Red as she did these things. She told him about everything she was doing and why it was important for her to do them.

Little Red was a good student for Andy. With Misty Dawn's help, he learned fast. Andy was very happy with how fast Little Red was learning. She had thought that time was going to be a problem. Because Little Red was such a good student, time became less of a problem.

Soon the time would come when Little Red would have to get used to a rider on his back. That was something new for him to learn, and it was something very important for him to learn. Soon, Andy was able to saddle and ride Little Red.

John and Andy spent some important time building a wooden machine. The machine was made of two-by-four wood studs and plywood. It looked and worked like the metal starting gate at the racetrack. They painted it a dark green so that it was the same color as the starting gate at the track. They wanted the machine to look as much like a starting gate as they could.

After Andy had ridden Little Red around the meadow sitting in the saddle and holding onto the reigns of the bridle, it was time to start teaching him about the starting gate. Andy wanted to teach Little Red how to start out of the gate as fast as possible.

The first few strides of the race were very important. When the gate sprang open, Little Red had to be ready to make those first few strides perfectly. Andy knew that racehorses lost races because they could not overcome a bad start.

Little Red must learn how to always get a good start. She knew that a good start began with the jockey and the horse thinking with one mind. The horse had to be alert. The horse's ears had to be up. His eyes had to be bright. He had to be looking straight ahead at the doors of the starting gate. Every muscle had to be tensed and every nerve had to be alert for the start. The horse had to be ready to spring forward at the very first second that the doors of the gate flew open. The jockey had to be ready for this jump by his horse.

From the start to the finish, the jockey and the horse had to work together like a perfectly oiled machine. Each piece of a perfect machine worked together to make the machine do what it should be doing. The jockey had to guide the horse around the track. The jockey did this by a small pull on the reigns on one side of the horse's head or the other. In that way, the horse under him knew which way to go. The jockey got the horse to run slower by pulling back on both of the reigns. That was the jockey's job. The horse's job was to run as fast as the jockey wanted and to have the strength to be able to run the fastest at the end of the race.

During a race, trouble could come from many places. The jockey had to watch out for possible trouble and help his horse to avoid it. Horses could be bunched up in front of him and the jockey would have to find a way to guide his horse around that group of horses. Horses in front of him could suddenly slow down and he would have to be ready to move his horse out of their way.

When John and Mary had finished the gate, Andy and her mother would practice with it. Mary would pull hard on the rope and at the same time ring the starting bell. The front doors of the gate would fly open using springs. While Mary practiced with the rope and the bell, Andy held Little Red's bridle so that he could watch what was going on. After a few times, Andy saddled up Misty Dawn and put her into the wooden gate. Little Red watched as his mother broke out of the starting gate when the doors flew open. He watched as she started out of the gate like a good racehorse should.

After watching Misty Dawn start out of the gate many times, Andy was sure that Little Red was ready to try it. Being inside the starting gate felt funny to Little Red. With Andy in the saddle, Little Red was led into the gate by John. The front doors of the gate were already closed. The sides of the gate were so close that Little Red could not move from one side to the other. When he was all of the way into the gate, his nose almost touched the front doors. Then the back doors of the gate were closed. Little Red felt like he was pinned up in a very little room. He did not like that feeling.

Andy knew what Little Red was feeling. She patted her horse on his neck and talked to him in a low soothing voice. She told Little Red not to worry. She told him that he would not be hurt in the gate. Little Red knew from watching his mother that soon the front doors of the gate would fly open and the bell would ring.

Even though Little Red knew what was going to happen, he still jumped with fright when the doors sprang open. Andy did not rush him out of the gate. Instead, she let him walk out on his own. She let him walk slowly around to the back of the gate. Once again, Little Red was loaded into the gate. Once again, he was closed into the small space and once again the front doors of the gate sprang open. Over and over, Andy, John, and Mary practiced with Little Red and the starting gate.

As Fall turned to Winter and the days grew colder, and shorter, Little Red got better and better in the starting gate. Finally, when the doors sprang open, Andy would rush her horse out just like in a real race. Each time, however, she would stop Little Red and turn him back toward the rear of the gate to do it all over again. Over and over in the bone chilling cold, the practices went on.

The Winter continued to get colder and Little Red continued to get better in the starting gate. It was like magic. Little Red was so good that it was almost as though he knew when the gate was going to open. He was getting a sixth sense about the timing of the gate's opening.

As Winter began to come to an end, Andy was ready to start practicing the whole race with Little Red. When the gate sprang open and the bell rang, Little Red was ready. Andy was also ready. Out of the gate they rushed. They raced smoothly around the meadow. On the first few times, Andy let Little Red run easily and slowly. However, as the days went by, Andy made Little Red run faster and harder and longer.

Over time, Andy also slowly increased the amount of weight Little Red had to carry on his back. She did this by adding little weights to the saddle to make it heavier. The more weight Little Red could carry, the stronger he would be.

John had been busy all winter, too. When not helping to school Little Red in the starting gate, he was working in a factory in town. The money John earned helped to pay some of the farm's bills. John had also gone back to the bank and gotten another loan.

Spring was on the way and Andy felt sure that her colt was ready. Misty Dawn had watched all of this training for her son. She, too, was sure that her son was ready to race.

Chapter Nine

Once again Spring returned to the bluegrass of Kentucky. Once again it was a special time for Richland Stables. Finally, the cold practicing in the big meadow was over. Finally, it was time to move Red Dawn to a stall in a barn at Keeneland Racetrack.

John and Andy moved Little Red to Keeneland in the old truck. They made the move two weeks before racing was to start. Andy wanted Little Red to get used to the sights and the sounds of a real racetrack.

There were no special barns for special horses at the track now. All of the stalls looked alike. All of them were nice, but none of them were fancy. Even so, Red Dawn's stall at the track was far better than the one he had been in the old barn at Richland Stables.

Each morning at dawn, Andy exercised Little Red. Each day, for the two weeks before racing started, Little Red and Andy practiced in the real starting gate at the track. Little Red practiced with other two-year-old horses. None of these horses had ever been on a racetrack before.

Little Red noticed that the real starting gate was a lot like the one he had used at the farm. But the real starting gate had spaces and doors for fourteen horses at one time. Little Red loved to hear the sound of the gates snapping open and the starting bell ringing.

Red Dawn also noticed that the dirt at the track was very different from the dirt at the farm. The dirt on the track was very, very soft and very smooth. Sometimes, when he was running on the grass in the meadow, he would step on a rock and hurt his hoof. Little Red did not have to worry about rocks on the racetrack. It felt great to run on the very soft, smooth dirt. He felt like he could run all day without being tired. The dirt of the track and the sights and sounds of the track gave him energy. Little Red was sure that he would love racing.

Andy was listed as Red Dawn's trainer. She was the first woman to ever be listed as a trainer in Kentucky. John and Mary Bell from Richland Stables were listed as the owners of Red Dawn.

There was still a lot to do before Little Red could race. The jockey who would ride him had to have a special shirt and cap. Each horse owner had their own special colors and designs for those shirts and caps. These different colors and designs helped the track announcer in the stands to tell one horse from another from a long distance away. In that way, the announcer could then tell the crowd in the stands how the race was going.

Mary looked at Richland Stables "silks," as the shirts and caps were called. They had hung in the attic of their home since the day Misty Dawn had run her last race. The silks were faded and looked worn.

Little Red was the start of a new day for Richland Stables. He had to carry a jockey with new silks. Mary bought the material at the store and started sewing the new silks herself.

Richland Stables colors were blue, as light as the sky in the Spring, and white, as bright as sunny clouds in summer. Mary sewed the light blue material into a jockey's shirt. Onto the shirt, she sewed Richland Stables' special design. Across the back of the shirt was a big white cross. The shirt buttoned up the front and at the neck was a white silky bow tie. The cap was light blue all over. Mary didn't actually make a jockey's helmet. She made a cloth covering for the helmet that all of the jockeys used. The jockey needed the helmet to protect their head. Before each race the jockey would put the owner's cover onto his helmet and put on the owner's silks.

During the day of races, a jockey could race many different horses in many different races for many different owners. Jockeys would change silks for each race.

Andy had to find a jockey to ride Little Red in his first race. Jockeys cost money. Each time a jockey rode a horse in a race, the owners had to pay him a riding fee. While the fee was the same for all jockeys, good jockeys only rode on good horses. In addition to getting a riding fee, if the horse he was riding won money by winning the race, the jockey would get part of that money from the owners. Horses won the most money by coming in first in a race. The horses won less money for coming in second and even less money for coming in third. Finally, the least amount of money was won by a horse coming in fourth. Horses that finished after fourth did not win any money.

It was expensive racing a horse. The feed for the horse had to be bought from the track and feed cost a lot of money. Horses eat a lot of feed. Also, the riding fee had to be paid regardless of whether his horse won the race or not.

The winnings for the horses were called a "purse." Races that were not very important and did not have many horses entered into them had small purses. Important races had larger purses.

Races for two-year-old horses who were just starting in racing had small purses. It was this kind of race that was going to be Little Red's first race at Keeneland.

It had already cost Richland Stables five hundred dollars in fees and feed bills for Little Red. A horse could only run every ten days or so when the races are not very long. When the horses are racing in longer races, they had to rest several more days before racing again. If Little Red did not win his first race, it would be ten more days before he could try again. Meanwhile, the feed bills would continue to mount up.

The bank had told John that they could not loan him any more money. Richland Stables did not have much money left. Little Red had to start winning right away.

Andy was sure that Little Red would win. Red Dawn was sure he would win. John and Mary knew that he HAD to win.

Chapter Ten

The day of Red Dawn's first race began grey and rainy. It had rained all night. The soft, smooth dirt of the track had turned to a sea of water and mud. It was not the bright, sunny day that Andy hoped it would be. Red Dawn was entered in the second race of the day. It was a short race just for horses that were new to racing. The race was five furlongs in length. The racetrack was one mile around. The track was divided into eight equal imaginary sections. Each section was called a furlong. That meant that Red Dawn would be running in a race that was a little more than a half of a mile in length.

Little Red had run much longer distances in the big meadow on the farm. When Misty Dawn and he had raced around the meadow, the distance had been about a half of a mile; this distance should be easy for Little Red. However, in a short race like this, the start was more important than ever. He knew that a bad start could put him so far behind that he would not have the time to catch up to the horses in front of him.

In the same race as Little Red, there was a horse named Bluegrass King. This horse had been one of the horses that had been sold for one million dollars at the same yearling sales where he had been. Bluegrass King was now owned by Regal Farms. Because Bluegrass King was a special horse, Regal Farms took special care of him. His owner and trainer were sure that he would be the winner of the Kentucky Futurity in one year.

Also, in the race with Little Red was another million-dollar horse. He was owned by a California farm called Sandstone Farms. Windward was the name of this horse and his owners were also sure he would win the Kentucky Futurity in one year.

The Kentucky Futurity was only for three-year-old horses. It was held on the first Saturday in May every year at Miles Park in Louisville, Kentucky. It was the most important horse race in America for thoroughbred horses. A horse that won the Kentucky Futurity would be considered very special for the rest of his life.

Each of the horses that were starting their racing lives on that rainy day at Keeneland hoped to be in the Kentucky Futurity in one year. That was a horse's dream. That was a trainer's dream and that was an owner's dream. It was Little Red's dream and it was Andy's dream.

For all of those horses, the first step in realizing that dream would come at the opening of the starting gate in the second race on that rainy day at Keeneland. It was an important first step. It could not be a bad step. For any of the horses in the race, a bad step here and the road to the Kentucky Futurity would become a little harder.

As the first race of the day was starting, Andy heard the announcement she had waited months to hear. "Trainers get your horses ready for the second race please."

Just as soon as the first race ended, Andy walked Red Dawn out of his stall and toward the saddling area. For each horse and each race, the same things were always done. The horses were led to the saddling area, called the "paddock." There, a track official would check each horse's tattooed number to make sure the right horse was in the race. Then the trainers would put the saddle cloth on their horse. This number was usually the horse's gate number and it helped the people in the stands to identify the horse. Then the saddle was put on the horse. At that point the jockeys would meet with the trainers to talk about the horse and the race.

Andy met with her jockey, who didn't say anything. Andy said, "Red Dawn is a very smart horse. He is fast and loves to run. Let him run the way he wants to run. If you just keep him from being blocked by other horses, he will win this race for you."

Still the jockey, Mike Jones, did not say anything. However, he did wonder to himself how Andy had gotten to be a trainer. She was nothing but a young girl. He thought, "What does she know about racing."

Andy warned him, "Just be ready for the start. This horse has a sense about when the gate is going to fly open. At the very second the gate opens; he will rush out of it with a jump. Be ready for it."

Jones said, "I know what to do. I know how to ride a racehorse."

Just then the track official said, "Riders up."

As all trainers do, Andy boosted the jockey up into Little Red's saddle. There was no more time to talk. Andy could only hope that Mike Jones had listened closely to what she had said.

With ten minutes to go before the start of the race, the jockeys rode their horses onto the track. As the horses trotted slowly around the track to warm up, Andy ran up into the stands. She wanted to be with her parents to watch Little Red's first race. John and Mary had placed a bet on Red Dawn. They had bet that Red Dawn would win the race. Although John and Mary were not people who normally bet on horses, they felt like they had to bet on their own horse. They bet ten dollars to win on Red Dawn. If Little Red did win the race, they would win a lot more money than they had bet. If he came in second, or worse, they would not win any money at all.

John and Mary held hands nervously as they watched Little Red trot around the track in the rain. All of those cold hours practicing in the big meadow were on their minds as they watched. This was the beginning. The was the new start for Richland Stables.

Chapter Eleven

As the time got closer to the start of the race, the jockeys guided their horses behind the starting gate. At five furlongs, the gate was set up about halfway down the backside of the track. The race would be a short run through the rest of the back stretch. Then the horses would run into the wide turn on the way to the long straight part of the track called the "stretch." Toward the end of the stretch was the finish line. After easily running down the back stretch and through the final turn, the horses would start to run as fast as they could down the stretch toward the finish line, or the "wire." It was sometimes called a "wire" because high above the track an actual thick wire was stretched across the track to mark the end of the race.

There were eight horses entered in this second race of the day, including Red Dawn. The official starter stood on a little platform near the starting gate. It was the starters' job to get all of the horses into the gate on time. The starter had helpers actually on the track. Their job was to lead the horses into the gates. One of the helpers stood up in the gate holding the horse's bridle to try to keep his head looking straight. The starter's most important job was to give each horse a fair start. The starter did this by watching each horse closely while they went in the gate. Once the horse had been put into the gate, another helper would close the back doors to the gate. When all of the horses were standing still and looking forward, the starter would push a little button in his hand.

All eight horses were loaded into the starting gate without any trouble. On one side of Little Red was Bluegrass King. On the other side of Little Red was Windward.

Red Dawn knew that both of those horses were thinking that they were better than he was. Both of them thought that he was just a poor little horse from a poor little farm. They laughed at him and made fun of him. They were going to make him eat the mud that would be flying up from their hooves as they raced in front of him. They were both sure that they would be running in the front of all of the horses and he would be running in the back of all of them.

Little Red's ears were up, and his eyes were sharp and bright. He was looking straight at the front doors of the gate. When those doors opened, he would be ready. He would show all of the other horses just who he was. He would especially show Bluegrass King and Windward that he was not some poor little horse from a poor little farm. He would show them that he was the best horse in the race.

All of that happened in the few seconds that all of the horses were standing still in the gate. Everything was ready. The starter watched each horse closely. He pushed the button. With a loud bang all of the front doors of the gate flew open and the bell rang loudly.

Red Dawn was ready for all of that to happen. However, Mike Jones, his jockey, was not. When the gate flew open, Red Dawn sprang out with a big jump. Because Jones was not leaning forward over Red Dawn's head. He was thrown backward in the saddle. He yanked back on the reigns to try to catch himself so that he wouldn't fall off the back of his horse. That jerked Red Dawns head up into the air.

All of the other horses started out of the gate with a rush. Little Red tried to run with them but his jockey kept tugging back on his reigns. He kept thinking, "What is the matter? We have got to be running fast."

But his jockey was still unsteady in the saddle. Along with feeling that he was going to fall off of his horse, Jones was having trouble seeing through the rain and the mud, which was being thrown up on him by all of the horses in front of him.

Little Red was confused. He did not know what the matter was. He kept thinking, "Let me run." But still his jockey held him back. He tried to catch up to the horses in front of him. He found that hard to do when the jockey kept pulling back on his head. He knew that a horse and a jockey had to work like a perfect machine. Mike Jones and Little Red were not working like a perfect machine. While Little Red wanted to win the race, Mike Jones just wanted to keep from falling off of his horse.

Bluegrass King won the race. Windward came in second. Red Dawn came in last.

Andy was mad and Little Red was frustrated. Andy ran down to the track to see the jockey. After the jockey had jumped off of Red Dawn, Andy asked, "What kind of race was that? What happened to you?"

Jones said, "What do you mean? You have a crazy horse here."

Andy answered, "Why didn't you let him run? He should have won that race."

"Let him run?" Jones said angrily, "he almost threw me off of him at the start. He is crazy. He has a mind of his own. I couldn't control him."

"My horse should have won that race and you made him lose it," Andy replied.

Mike Jones said again, "That horse of yours is crazy. He almost killed me. I won't ride him again. And after I get done telling all of the other jockeys about him, I don't think any of the others will want to ride him either."

Andy said, "Red Dawn doesn't need a jockey like you. He needs a jockey as good as HE is."

The jockey had heard enough from some young trainer who didn't know what she was doing and with a crazy horse that had almost killed him. The jockey turned and walked away toward the jockey's quarters. Jones didn't care about Red Dawn or his trainer. He was just happy to be alive.

Andy led Little Red slowly back toward the barns. As they walked past the stands, Little Red and Andy heard some shouts of "Boo" from the people who had lost money by betting on him. Andy had a lot to think about. What was she going to do now?

Chapter Twelve

Andy worked on cleaning the mud off of Little Red while John and Mary looked on sadly. This was another sad day for Richland Stables. It was a day like many of the other sad days in the past. The day had started out with hope and happiness, but it had ended up in despair and sadness.

Even in the sadness, Andy was not going to give up. Little Red was a good horse, she knew it. Andy knew in her heart that he should have won that race. With the right jockey riding on him, he would have won the race. She saw that Little Red had not given up on the track. Even with a bad jockey, he had tried to win the race. She saw that he had not given up even when he had no chance to win. She knew that was a sign of a champion.

Mike Jones did not understand Little Red. Andy was afraid that he was going to give Little Red a bad name. He was going to tell all of the other jockeys not to ride Red Dawn.

What was Andy going to do? She understood Little Red. Why couldn't the other people understand him like she did? She felt like she could read his mind and she also felt like Little Red could understand what she was saying and thinking. She understood Little Red and Little Red understood her. They made a great team. She thought, "That is what it takes for a horse and a jockey to work like a well-oiled machine. They have to think like one mind."

With that, Andy knew what she had to do. She would ride Red Dawn herself. She would be his trainer and his jockey. She had exercised horses for years. She knew how to be a jockey. Because she understood Little Red, she would be the best jockey he could ever have. They were going to run in races like a well-oiled machine.

Andy's decision to ride Red Dawn was a very good one, for several reasons. It put the best possible jockey on Red Dawn. It saved the farm the riding fees for a jockey. And when they won the races, they would not have to share the purse with another person. Little Red would win, Andy was sure of that.

Soon, Little Red was clean and dry and back in his stall. Andy then ran over to the Racing Secretary's office. She entered Red Dawn in a six-furlong race. It was a race only for two-year-old horses who had never won a race. Andy told the Racing Secretary that she was going to be the trainer AND the jockey on Red Dawn.

The day of Red Dawn's next race dawned clear and sunny. Andy was sure that it was going to be the start of a great day. It was going to be a great day for her horse, for her farm, and for her family.

Dressed in the sky blue and white silks of Richland Stables, Andy rode Little Red onto the track for the race. Everyone in the stands at the racetrack could bet on any horse in the race. They could bet the horse to win the race, or to come in second in the race, or to come in third in the race. There were many ways they could bet on the horse they liked.

Because Red Dawn had come in last in his only other race, very few people bet on him to win the race. John and Mary were going to bet on him to win because they knew that he was going to win. They took twenty dollars and bet it on Red Dawn to win the race. Because so few people were betting on him and so many were betting on the other horses, if he did win, John and Mary could win a lot of money.

John and Mary watched the "Tote Board." This was an electronic board with lights that formed numbers so that everyone in the stands could read them. The numbers showed the "odds" for each horse in the race. The "odds" were a guess at how much money a bettor could win by betting correctly on any particular horse. As more and more money was bet on the different horses in the race, the "odds" were constantly changing. The tote board showed that if Red Dawn were to win the race, John and Mary would win one hundred dollars for every two dollars they had bet.

Everything was riding on Red Dawn's shoulders in this race. There really were no other chances left for their farm. All of the money had run out. The race was the last chance to save the farm. The winning horse's share of the purse was over ten thousand dollars. Mary and John knew that. Andy knew it, and Little Red knew it as well.

Andy and Little Red were ready. Little Red stood quietly in the starting gate. He was alert and ready to jump out of the gate the instant the doors flew open in front of him. Andy leaned forward in the saddle and closer to Little Red's neck.

A split second before the starter pushed the button to release the gates, a voice inside Little Red's mind said, "Now!" He rushed forward just as the gates flew open in front of him. He had beaten all of the horses out of the starting gate. Andy and Little Red ran like a well-oiled machine around the track. He ran on as he heard the cheering crowd in the stands. The roar of the crowd sounded like the roar of the wind or the crashing of giant ocean waves. Andy kept her head down next to Little Red's neck. She kept saying over and over, "Come on, boy. Keep going, you are going to win!"

Red Dawn ran like he had never run before. He ran much faster than he had ever run in the big meadow. It felt wonderful to have Andy riding on his back again. It felt wonderful to have Andy talking to him as they ran. To him it felt like he was flying. He could not feel his hooves beating into the soft dirt track. He felt so good.

Red Dawn and Andy won the race. John, Mary and Andy along with Richland Stables won the purse of over ten thousand dollars. John took most of the money to the bank the very next day. He was able to pay off some of his old bills and some of his old loans. The farm kept five hundred dollars to pay the cost of keeping Little Red at the track to enter other races.

Before the racing meet was over at Keeneland, Red Dawn and Andy had won another race. After that race, the farm had over twelve thousand dollars from the winning purse. John was able to pay off more old loans and to pay some of the old tax bills on the farm. Everything was looking good for Little Red and Richland Stables.

At the end of the racing season at Keeneland, Andy moved Little Red to Miles Park in Louisville. This was the old, famous racetrack that was the home of the Kentucky Futurity.

Even though Little Red was only a two-year-old and could not run with the three-year-old horses in the Kentucky Futurity, he did race on Futurity Day.

Richland Stables still needed more money to pay off all of its debts and to finish paying off the tax bills. John, Mary, and Andy thought that it was time to enter Red Dawn in a race with a bigger purse. Andy entered Red Dawn in the third race on Futurity Day. It was a seven-furlong claiming race for two-year-old horses.

A claiming race was a common type of race for thoroughbred racehorses. A value was placed on all of the horses who wanted to run in the race. In the race Red Dawn was in, the value of the horses was placed at twenty-five thousand dollars. If a horse owner wanted to buy one of the horses in the race, all the owner had to do was to put his name and the horse's name in the claiming box before the race started. Then when the race was over, that owner owned the horse and paid the value of the horse to the old owner. The old owner also got to keep the purse if the horse won the race. However, if something happened to the horse during the race, such as getting hurt, the new owner still had to pay for the horse and still owned the horse.

It was a gamble both ways. Some owners put their horses in claiming races for the bigger purses with the hope that no one would claim their horse. Andy did not think her horse would be claimed. "After all," she thought, "even though he has won two races, he lost his first race by a long distance." However, it would not take good horse people long to notice a good horse. It also would not take horse betters from noticing a good horse, as well.

In the third race on Futurity Day, Richland Stables won the purse of twenty thousand dollars. It also got twenty-five thousand dollars because Red Dawn had been claimed.

Bill Sims of Stardust Racing Stables had put his name and Red Dawn's name in the claiming box before the race.

Richland Stables was now out of debt. All of the bills had been paid. But, most importantly, Richland Stables was out of racing. Red Dawn was gone.

Chapter Thirteen

The ride back to the farm from Louisville was one of the longest rides John, Mary, and Andy had ever taken. It was a ride filled with questions. Each person in the old truck wondered, "What will we do now?" During that ride, Andy made up her mind that she would go and see Misty Dawn in the old barn.

As soon as Andy walked into the barn, Misty Dawn knew something was very wrong. Andy's eyes were sad looking. She did not hold her head up proudly. Misty Dawn thought, "What could be the matter?"

Andy walked over to Misty Dawn and patted her gently on her neck. She really did not know how to begin. Finally, she said, "Well, Misty, we lost Little Red today."

Misty Dawn raised her head up with a start. Her mind was filled with questions. She thought, "What does that mean? Did Little Red break his leg in a race? Was he so badly injured that he wouldn't live?"

Those are fears that all racehorses live with. The bones in their legs are very small compared to how big their body is. Those bones could break easily. A misstep on the track and a bone could break. In most cases the break was so bad that the horse could not continue to live. All Misty Dawn could think was "How was he lost?" She was frantic with worry about her son.

Andy could understand Misty Dawn's worry. She went on, "Little Red was claimed in a race today. We don't own him anymore. He won't be coming back here after the racing season in over. He is now owned by Stardust Racing Stables."

Misty Dawn was relieved at least. She thought, "He is alive and healthy." She knew how the claiming system worked. But she would not give up hope. She still hoped that she would see her son again.

Andy could now see that Misty Dawn was more relaxed. She said, "Little Red was our future. He was such a good horse. I am afraid I don't see any way of getting him back. Bill Sims is never going to sell him and probably won't ever put him in another claiming race."

Andy turned to walk out of the barn. She had one more thing to say to Misty Dawn. She said, "I am going to watch every race that Little Red is in. I promise you that he is going to be treated the way he deserves to be treated."

Andy had her chance to watch Red Dawn race just fourteen days later. Stardust entered Red Dawn in a seven furlong Allowance Race. This was not a claiming race. Bill Sims was not going to take a chance on losing Red Dawn to a claim.

Allowance races were for better horses than horses that run in claiming races. Red Dawn was moving up in the eyes of the horse owners.

Red Dawn was one of the favorites in the race. Most of the betters were betting on Red Dawn to win the race. Andy bet some money on Red Dawn to win the race. But she had bet the money more out of love for her horse than the hope that he would be winning some money.

The race was a bad experience for Little Red. Little Red did not like the feeling of someone else on his back. He was restless in the starting gate. The voice in his head did not tell him when to start. He wasn't the first horse out of the gate. He ran faster than the other horses in the race. But he and his jockey did not work like a well-oiled machine. Little Red found himself blocked by the horses in front of him and beside him. He tried very hard to get though those horses, but the jockey did not help him find the best way to do that.

Red Dawn came in sixth in the race. He had been beaten again by Bluegrass King. He had also been beaten by Windward, who had come in second in the race. Back in the horse barns, both Bluegrass King and Windward laughed at him. They still called him just a poor, little horse. They both thought, "He will never be able to win against the big boys like us."

Each race that Red Dawn was in seemed to prove that they were right. Each allowance race that Red Dawn was in turned out to be a bad experience for him. In each of the races, something seemed to happen to keep him from winning. In each of the races, Little Red tried as hard as he could. Even though he never gave up, he always ended up losing at the end of the race.

As the Fall racing season began again at Keeneland, Bill Sims began to have doubts about Red Dawn. He thought, "Maybe the horse had an injury that kept him from winning." He had the vet check him out, but nothing was found. The other horse people began to wonder about Red Dawn, too. Bluegrass King and Windward, who always seemed to be racing at the same tracks that he was racing at, continued to mock him.

Bill Sims started entering Red Dawn into claiming races again. He wanted to try to find a race that Red

Dawn could win. To do that, he had to enter him in races with slower horses.

Finally, in Red Dawn's second race of the fall meet at Keeneland, he was entered into a five thousand dollar claiming race. This was Andy's chance. She ran to the bank for a five-thousand-dollar loan. She knew why Little Red could not win. She knew he wasn't injured. Little Red's problems always started with the jockeys. The jockeys just did not understand Red Dawn, but she did.

Andy put her name and Red Dawn's name in the claiming box before the race. No matter what happened in that race, Red Dawn would belong to Richland Stables again.

Red Dawn came in fourth in the race. But now he belonged to Andy and Richland Stables. Andy returned him home to the barn at Richland Stables. Now Andy was happy, Little Red was happy, and Misty Dawn was happy.

Right then, a plan started to form in Andy's mind. It was an important plan. It was a plan to make Red Dawn the most famous racehorse in America.

Chapter Fourteen

Andy started working on her plan the very next day. She drove to Louisville and went to Miles Park. She officially made Red Dawn eligible to run in the Kentucky Futurity. To sign him up for the Futurity cost three hundred dollars. A horse could only run in the Futurity on the first Saturday in May, but he had been entered before January first. Since the initial cost of entry was so cheap and the race was so important, many, many horse owners entered their horses in the Kentucky Futurity. Most horses that would be entered would never prove good enough to actually run in the Futurity, but by the end of a horse's second year of age, the owners did not know that.

The list of the horses eligible to run in the Futurity was published in the newspaper. There were three hundred and fifty horses on the list. Red Dawn's name was there. Bluegrass King and Windward's names were also on the list.

The first part of Andy's plan was over. Her horse was eligible to run in the Kentucky Futurity. As the actual date for the running of the race grew closer, the cost of keeping a horse eligible to run got higher and higher. Because of this rise in costs, the owners started looking harder and harder at their horses. To actually enter the race, the cost was ten thousand more dollars and to actually start a horse in the race the owners had to pay another twenty-five thousand dollars. The entry cost had to be paid the week before the Futurity and the starting fee had to be paid Futurity Day morning. The money collected by the track from the owners of the starting horses was added to the purse for the Futurity. The winning horse got most of those fees plus most of the three hundred and fifty thousand dollars provided by Miles Park.

Winning the Kentucky Futurity would mean everything to Richland Stables. However, Richland Stables had to have the additional money needed to enter and start Red Dawn. That meant Little Red had to win at least one other race.

The Kentucky Futurity was one mile and a quarter long. It would have been the very first time any of the three-year-old horses in the race would have been asked to run that far. For that reason, everyone knew that the Kentucky Futurity would help prove who was a really good horse and who was not.

Andy knew something important about Little Red. She had watched him race a mile and a quarter with Misty Dawn in the meadow. When Little Red had raced his mother in the meadow, he was younger and weaker. However, at the same time, he was also not carrying a jockey and some extra weights on his back when he ran. Andy had to be sure that Little Red was strong enough to go the distance of the Futurity. She had to know that Little Red could run like the wind along with her.

She was sure Little Red was ready. It was time for the third part of her plan. She moved Red Dawn to a stall at Keeneland Racetrack. The excitement of the Spring Racing Meet was starting.

Most of the horses that might be running in the Futurity were already racing in other parts of the country. Every trainer had his own idea of how to get a horse ready for the Futurity. During the winter, most trainers took their horses to Florida or California to train and run. The horses that were good enough to run in the Futurity did not come back to Kentucky until two weeks before the actual race.

Regal Farms had taken Bluegrass King to Florida. There he won every race he had entered. So, he was the favorite to win the Futurity even before the racing started in the Spring.

Another popular horse for the Futurity was Windward. Sandstone Farms had taken him to

California to train and race. The owners of Windward did not want to run against Bluegrass King until they were in the last big race together. Two times Windward had raced against Bluegrass King as a two-year-old horse and each time he had lost. He had always been close, but still, he had always lost.

Little Red had also raced against those two horses and each time he had lost badly. He had lost to them in his very first race and had lost to them in an allowance race. He had also lost to one or the other of them in other races while being owned by Bill Sims.

Andy did not want to race against them again until they were together in the Kentucky Futurity. That would be the showdown.

Once housed in the stall at Keeneland, it was time for the fourth part of Andy's plan. She walked into Keeneland's Racing Secretary's office. She told the racing secretary that she was Red Dawn's trainer and jockey again. She told the secretary that she was ready to start racing him again.

The racing secretary told her that he was happy for her. The secretary said, "What race are you going to start him in, Andy? We have a nice seven furlong race for three-year-olds coming up next week. How about that one?"

Andy shook her head. "No. We're running in the Bluegrass Stakes."

Chapter Fifteen

The Bluegrass Stakes was one of the several most important races a horse could win on the way to the Kentucky Futurity. At one time, the winner of the Bluegrass Stakes was usually the favorite in the Kentucky Futurity. There was a time when the winner of the Bluegrass Stakes was usually also the winner of the Futurity. However, in more recent years, that was not happening.

Trainers and owners believe in good luck and bad luck. If they saw the winner of one particular race also doing well in the Futurity year after year, they also wanted their horse to run in that same race before the Futurity. So, in more recent years, most horses that intended to run in the Futurity were not running in the Bluegrass Stakes. Some trainers thought there were not enough days between the two races to give their horses a chance to rest before having to run a mile and a quarter.

But Andy did not agree with those trainers and owners. She was sure that Little Red could win the Bluegrass Stakes and the Futurity too. Andy wanted to show everyone that a good horse could do that. She and Little Red were going to show everyone that they could make their own good luck through hard work.

The Bluegrass Stakes was one mile and one eighth long. While it was an eighth of a mile shorter than the Futurity, it would still be the longest distance any of the horses in that race would have run up to that point. It would be the most important race of Little Red's life thus far. Andy and Little Red needed the large purse from the Bluegrass Stakes to be able to pay the entry fee and the starting fee for the Futurity.

The day that the Bluegrass Stakes was run, the weather was sunny, warm, and beautiful. It was a perfect day for racing in Kentucky. There were ten horses entered into the race, including Red Dawn.

Finally, everything was ready for the start of the Bluegrass Stakes. Andy was sitting on Little Red in the starting gate. John and Mary had bet fifty dollars on Red Dawn to win.

The starter pushed the button and the doors of the starting gate flew open. Little Red jumped out of the gate ahead of all of the other horses. The voice in his head was working again.

Since the track was one mile around, the starting gate was set just a furlong before the place where the race would end after the horses had gone all the way around the track.

It was important to Andy and Little Red not to be squeezed into the rail as the horses ran through the first turn and into the back stretch of the racetrack. After the back stretch came the final turn before heading down the final stretch and to the wire.

At the start of the race, Red Dawn was in front of the other horses. The roar of the crowd was in Little Red's ears as they ran past the stands for the first time. Andy wanted Little Red to run easily from the start. She knew that this was a long race and running too fast at the beginning may use up Little Red strength before the race was over. She wanted to make sure he had enough strength for the end of the race.

Andy settled Little Red into an easy run around the first turn. Two other horses were running beside him. Down the back stretch, five horses ran as a group ahead of the others. Red Dawn was leading this group by the length of his neck.

Andy felt good about Little Red and the way the race was going. She kept talking to Red Dawn. She kept telling him that he was going to win the race.

Moving though the final turn, everything looked good for Little Red's stretch run. Andy felt the power of Little Red's strides. Andy was sure he had enough strength left to win the race.

Red Dawn was just barely in the lead at the start of the stretch. The straight path to the finish line was ahead of him. Suddenly, one of the horses beside him, pushed him against the rail. Andy's leg was brushing against the rail. Little Red had to slow down suddenly to keep from falling. By the time Andy and Little Red were racing at full speed again, the other horse was in the lead. It was a fast race to the wire. Little Red gave the race every bit of his strength. But try as he might, he just could not catch the other horse.

Red Dawn came in second in the Bluegrass Stakes. His try for the Kentucky Futurity was not good enough. He had not given up. Even when he was in trouble when that horse bumped him, he had not given up. He had tried as hard as he could try, but still he lost the race. He felt sad for Andy. He had let Andy down. Andy had told him that he was going to win the race and he didn't win the race.

Keeneland was an old-fashioned racetrack. The people in charge of running the track liked to keep it that way. For that reason, there were no public address announcer on loudspeakers for the crowd in the stands. Because there was no speaker system, Little Red did not know that the judges of the race were reviewing how it had been run. The race would not be official until the judges had finished with their reviews.

Each race was watched by a group of judges, who knew all about horse racing. The judges wanted to make sure that the race was fair. A jockey and a horse could be punished for not running a fair race.

The judges wanted to talk to the jockey of the winning horse and they also wanted to talk to Andy. The judges watched the films of the race from several different views. The judges needed to know just what had happened in the last turn before the start of the stretch. This was known as an "inquiry." The race was not official until the judges were satisfied. After ten minutes of asking questions and watching the films, the judges were satisfied. The message on the tote board was changed from "inquiry" to "official." The winner of the race was changed to Red Dawn because the horse that finished ahead of him in the race had interfered with him.

The judges had decided that Red Dawn would probably have won the race if the other horse had not bumped him. Because that other horse had caused Red Dawn to lose, that horse had been punished. That horse was moved from winning the race to being placed third.

When the change was flashed on the big board, a great cheer went up from the crowd in the stands. Red Dawn was a winner again. And he was on his way to Miles Park in Louisville, Kentucky and the Kentucky Futurity!

Chapter Sixteen

In the life of a thoroughbred racehorse and that horse's trainer, there was no time quite as special as the week before the Kentucky Futurity. Now, Little Red and Andy would know that feeling of excitement. It was a thrilling time to be a racehorse. To Little Red, it seemed like there was electricity in the air. Every morning of the week sparkled with bright sunshine. Every day was filled with activity.

Red Dawn was put in barn number 41. That was a special barn reserved only for the horses that were going to be racing in the big race. Finally, Red Dawn would know what it felt like to be in a special barn and to be treated like a special horse. There were security guards all around the barn. Security was tight.

Hundreds of reporters from around the world swarmed onto the grounds of Miles Park. There were reporters from all of the big newspapers from around the country. There were television reporters with their cameramen watching each horse work out in the mornings on the track. There were radio reporters with their tape recorders asking the trainers and owners questions. There were photographers everywhere. Each photographer was trying to get a special picture that would tell the real story of the Futurity. Each of the reporters wanted to write or broadcast a good Futurity story.

There were twenty horses in the Futurity including Red Dawn. In the stall beside Red Dawn was Bluegrass King. Because Bluegrass King had won all of his races, he was the favorite to win the big race.

Because he was the favorite, all of the reporters and photographers wanted to see Bluegrass King. All of the reporters wanted to get a story from Bluegrass King's trainer. Over and over, Little Red listened to the same questions and the same answers. Bluegrass

King's trainer bragged about how his horse was the very best in the race. The trainer said that he was only worried about Windward. He didn't think any of the other horses had much of a chance to beat his horse. He did tell the reporters that he thought the race was going to be fast, if it wasn't rainy on Futurity Day. He also told them that he thought it might be a close race between his horse and Windward. He said he thought the Futurity was going to be a very good race. He ended by saying that he had no doubt that his horse was going to win.

The next horse on every reporter's list was Windward. Windward was known as the "California Horse." He had won most of his races in California. He was owned by a California farm. The reporters knew that by talking about the rivalry between the Kentuckian, Bluegrass King, and the Californian, Windward, would make for a very good Futurity story.

Windward's trainer was asked the same questions that Bluegrass King's trainer had heard. He also said that he thought the race would be fast and close. He also ended by saying that he had no doubt that his horse was going to win.

Bill Sims also had a horse entered in the Futurity. His horse was named Regal Prince. The reporters asked him all of the same questions as they had asked the other trainers. They asked him one more question. They wanted to know how it felt to be running his horse in the Futurity against a horse that he had lost in a claiming race to Andy Bell?

A few of the reporters wanted to talk to Andy. These reporters thought that Andy and Red Dawn made a good story. They asked Andy how it felt to be such a young trainer, and a girl, running a horse in the Kentucky Futurity? They asked her how it felt to be Red Dawn's trainer and jockey. They wanted to know how it felt to win the Bluegrass Stakes only because of a judge's decision. They wanted to know how a horse as small as Red Dawn could win the Futurity, and they wanted to know if Andy was scared about racing her little horse in a race with the "big boys."

Andy patiently answered each question. She did not get mad at the reporters. She knew they were just looking for a good Futurity story. But every time Andy finished her talk, she always said, "Red Dawn will beat the big Kentuckian and the big Californian. Red Dawn will win the Kentucky Futurity."

At ten o'clock on Thursday morning of Futurity week, the horses were officially entered into the race. Andy gave the Racing Secretary her ten thousand dollars to enter Red Dawn. After all, twenty horses were entered in the race, it was time to assign post positions for the Futurity.

Post positions were the order in which the horses stood in the starting gate. Numbers from one to twenty were put into a box. The entries were put into another box. No one could see the information on the entry forms. First a horse's entry form was pulled from the box and then a number was pulled from the other box. Whatever number was pulled from the box, that was the post position for that horse.

Luck played a part in the starting position for each horse. Some trainers thought that certain post positions were good, and some were not good. Good post positions were thought to be from four to ten. Bad positions were thought to be the first and second position and any outside of twelve.

Bluegrass King was drawn into post position six. Windward got post position ten. Regal Prince got post position fourteen. Red Dawn got post position one.

Thursday afternoon and all day Friday was spent talking to the reporters again. Each trainer was asked how he felt about his horse's post position. Each trainer gave his opinion about whether the position would help or hurt his horse. Only a very few reporters bothered to talk to Andy, now. It was too late in the week to waste time talking to the trainer of a horse that had no chance of winning the race. The reporters wanted to spend their time with the favorites.

As the sun set on Friday evening, the week before the Futurity ended. It had been a hectic week. There had been press conferences, a parade down the main street of the city. There had been hot air balloon races and even a steamboat race. The owners and trainers were all special guests at all of these events. Andy had not gone to any of them, however. She had decided to stay close to Little Red. This was not a party week for Andy and her horse. This was the week before the most important race of their lives.

When the sun rose again, it would be the sunrise for Futurity Day. Win or lose it was a sunrise that all of the Futurity Horses would never forget. Since only three-year-old horses could run in the Futurity, it was a special sunrise that those horses would only experience that one time.

It would be a special sunrise for Red Dawn. Sixty miles away, at Richland Stables, it would be a special sunrise for Misty Dawn as well.

All of the practices were over for Andy and Little Red. All of the work that Misty Dawn had done with her son to get him ready for this one day was over. All of the planning by Andy was over. For Andy, Misty Dawn, and Little Red, it had been very difficult to sleep on that Friday night. All of them excitedly waited for the dawn of Futurity Day.

Chapter Seventeen

The outside gates to Miles Park opened at eight o'clock in the morning on Futurity Day. Thousands of college students had slept outside the track on Friday night. As the gates opened these people and thousands more poured inside. After paying for admission, they went through an underground tunnel below the track to be in the infield. On Futurity Day the area inside the actual racing track was opened up to anyone who wanted to go in after paying for their ticket. Across the track, the stands held seating for over forty thousand other people to watch the races. Behind the stands, there were gardens and areas where even many more thousands of people could be for the races.

The first race on Futurity Day was at eleven o'clock. The Futurity was not set to start until five-thirty in the afternoon. By that time, there would be over one hundred thousand people inside Miles Park to watch the Kentucky Futurity. Because the race would be televised, millions more people would be watching the race on television. The Kentucky Futurity was the most watched horse race in the world.

The hours before the Futurity were filled with activity for Andy. She had to pay the starting fee. She had to groom Red Dawn. She wanted him to look his very best for the television cameras. She also had to talk to a few more television reporters. One of the reporters for the national television network that was going to be broadcasting the race interviewed Andy.

The reporter asked, "What do you think Red Dawn's chances are of winning this race?"

Andy answered, " I believe that he has a great chance to win."

The reporter went on, "Do you think his small size will hurt him in the race? After all, he is only fourteen hands high."

Andy said, "He may be small on the outside, but he is big where it counts. In a race of this sort, that is where it counts the most. He has a big heart and he has never given up in any of his races. Even when he was being beaten, he did not give up and he won't give up today."

The reporter continued, " I understand you call him 'Little Red'."

"Yes, that's my own special name for him," Andy said.

"Well, the very best of luck to you and Little Red, today," the reporter finished.

Andy only said, "Thank You." As she turned back to working on grooming her horse, she heard the reporter continue to talk to the camera.

"Red Dawn - or 'Little Red' - is he the little horse that can win it today? In other races, there have been other small horses. Only one of those small horses was ever able to win a Futurity. Will Little Red be only the second horse to do it? He will be running against two large horses, with long legs, and strong bodies. Will Bluegrass King and Windward make Little Red look even smaller than he is?"

The reporter went on, "In many ways, Little Red is just like millions of regular people. He was raised on a poor little farm. He worked long and hard for any success that he has had. No one has ever given him any respect. No one, but his trainer, young Andrea Bell, thinks that he has a chance of winning against those bigger stronger horses. He will be racing against horses that are already worth millions of dollars. When it was his turn to be sold at the yearling sales, no one but his family wanted him. In many ways he will be carrying the love of millions of regular, working-class Americans with him today. Can he carry the weight of all of that hope? I think he can. Because his trainer says that he has something that the other horses don't have. He has a big heart."

The reporter finished his report, "Little Red, the little man's horse in the Kentucky Futurity. He will have to run the race of his life today."

The reporter had liked Red Dawn's nickname. Once his report was broadcast on national television right before the race, everyone watching would know about him. All across the country, Little Red would be known and loved by all of the people who thought of themselves as being too small to be important.

Andy knew the problems that Little Red faced in the race. In her mind, she had pictured the race a hundred times. The start was very important. Because Little Red was in the first post position, she had two choices of what to do at the start. She could have Little Red start fast and try to be in the lead going into the first turn. The other thing she could do would be to ask Little Red to start slower and try to keep out of trouble.

Both choices caused problems for Andy and Little Red. Taking the lead at the start of a long race, like the Futurity, puts a lot of pressure on a horse. It is very hard to be in the lead for a whole mile and still have the strength to be running fast for the last one quarter of a mile down the stretch to the finish line. Almost no horses have ever led from start to finish in the Futurity. Any horse that had tried it just couldn't keep up the pace at the end, and usually ended up at the back of all of the horses.

By starting slower and letting the other horses run in front of him could be a big problem too. Little Red's path through the other nineteen horses in the race could be blocked. Little Red may not be able to find a way to get through or around the horses in front of him. He may have the speed and the heart to win but he might not ever have the chance to win.

Andy decided to do something that few other trainers had been daring enough to try. She decided to have Little Red try to lead the Futurity from start to finish. She knew that this was a very big chance to ask Little Red to take. He was running the longest, hardest race of his life. He was racing against horses that had beaten him before and he was starting from a bad post position.

Even with all of those problems, Andy was confident. She had the best horse in America and in just a few hours, she would have the chance to prove it. She was going to ask Little Red to do something that would be very, very hard. Some people would think that she was asking Little Red to do something that was impossible. At the same time, Andy was absolutely sure that Little Red would not let her down.

Chapter Eighteen

Finally, it was time to walk Little Red around the track to the paddock. The crowd was very, very large. Just walking around the outside of the track, John and Mary could hear the crowd noise. It was a very loud, excited hum. It sounded like a gigantic machine running at full speed. Waiting in the paddock was Andy in her riding sinks.

In the paddock, Andy kept patting Little Red on the neck. She was with her horse in paddock position one. She said to Little Red, "Stay calm, boy. This is it. This is our day. This is our race. I know you are going to win today. We just have to stay calm."

Andy was telling Little Red to stay calm, but she was having trouble staying calm herself. The crowd noise was everywhere. The cameras and reporters were everywhere. John and Mary hugged Andy and wished her "good luck." They both hugged Little Red around the neck and wished him "good luck" as well.

Finally, they could hear a gigantic roar from the crowd inside the track as the bugler blared out the "call to the post." All of the waiting was finally over. The years of waiting and worrying and practicing were finally over. It was time for Andy to ride Little Red through the tunnel and onto the track for the Kentucky Futurity.

It was a tradition of the Futurity that when the first hoof of the first Futurity horse stepped onto the dirt of the track, the band would start playing, "My Old Kentucky Home" by Stephen Foster. Since Red Dawn was the number one horse, it was his hoof that signaled the start of that famous song.

While there were many people from all over the country in the stands for the Futurity, each person sang the old song like it was their own. As all of the Futurity horses were paraded slowly onto the track, Red Dawn heard the singing.

The voices of over one hundred thousand people swelled together toward the end of the song.

"Weep no more my lady,
Weep no more today.
We will sing one song for,
My Old Kentucky Home.
For my Old Kentucky Home,
Far away."

Kentuckians and non-Kentuckians alike had a little tear in their eyes at the end of the old song. After that, a great cheer went up from the crowd. The sound of that cheer washed down onto the horses on the track like a giant ocean wave.

The track announcer read the names of each of the horses as they paraded slowly past the stands. Now it was time for the horses to start trotting slowly around the track. Little Red was amazed at what he saw. Everywhere he looked he saw a sea of faces. People seemed to be everywhere. He could find no part of the track that was not surrounded by people. He had never experienced anything that looked like that before. Andy patted Little Red on the neck and said, calmly, "Everybody is looking at you, Little Red, and you look great. You are going to run great, too. I know it."

All of the horses trotted around the track, warming up. Finally, they were behind the starting gate. The starting gate was positioned at the start of the stretch. It was one quarter of a mile from the finish line. That meant that all of the horses had to run under the finish line twice and in front of the stands twice.

Because Red Dawn was the number one horse, he was loaded into the starting gate first. The twentieth horse was loaded in at the same time. All of the other horses had to follow, two at a time. Andy leaned over to talk quietly into Little Red's ear. She said, "Little Red, we have got to start fast. We have got to lead the race into the first turn. We can't take a chance on being bumped into the rail, like before. But most of all, Little Red, we have got to be running the fastest of all at the end."

Little Red heard and understood what Andy was asking him to do. He had to run as fast as he could. He had to run like a well-oiled machine. His hooves had to move over the track like he was flying. He had to win the Kentucky Futurity.

Chapter Nineteen

With a loud bang and a jangle of the bell and a great roar from the massive crowd, the starting gates flew open. Little Red jumped out of the gate ahead of all of the other horses.

The television announcer said in an excited voice, "And -- they're off!! Red Dawn gets a great start and immediately takes the lead."

Andy's head was up next to Little Red's neck. She said to him, "great start, boy. Now let's keep it going."

The race down the stretch for the first time was met with a continuing cheer from the crowd. The TV announcer said, "It's a cavalry charge past the stands for the first time. All twenty horses are running close together. Red Dawn continues to lead. Passing under the wire for the first time, it is Red Dawn first -

followed by Bluegrass King in second and Windward in third."

As the horses started into the first turn, Red Dawn could feel Bluegrass King right on his outside. He was squeezing Little Red into the rail. Even so, Little Red would not give up his place on the track. He was better and stronger than Bluegrass King. Red Dawn continued around the first turn.

The TV announcer said, "Going into the first turn, Red Dawn still leads. Bluegrass King is still pressing him and is in second. Windward and the other horses are falling back. They are saving their energy for the long run ahead. It's Red Dawn and Bluegrass Kind battling for the lead."

Andy said to Little Red, "Don't let that horse bother you, boy. You are the best. Let's show him!"

As the horses rounded the turn and headed into the back stretch, Red Dawn and Bluegrass King raced together. Again, Bluegrass King tried to push Red Dawn into the rail. Andy turned and yelled to the jockey on Bluegrass King, "Hey, watch it! Keep your horse away from us."

The other jockey just yelled back, "Get out of our way. We are coming past you!"

But Red Dawn thought to himself, "No horse is getting in front of me today."

Into the back stretch, the two horses raced stride for stride; they were eye to eye and the two jockeys were side by side. The TV announcer said excitedly, "What a duel! What a race! Little Red Dawn and big Bluegrass King are right together down the back stretch. Neither horse is willing to give in. This is turning into one of the fastest Futurities in history!"

To Little Red it seemed quieter down the back stretch. The stands were all of the way across the track and infield. Little Red could hear Bluegrass King's hooves pounding into the soft dirt. He could hear Bluegrass King's breath rushing out in great loud bursts.

Red Dawn was flying like the wind in a bluegrass meadow. But his rival was right beside him. He could not get in front of Bluegrass King, no matter how fast he ran. Andy once again leaned down into Red Dawn's neck. She said, "All right Little Red, now it's time to show these other horses who you really are."

Little Red knew that he was trying with all of his might to do just that, but he just couldn't shake Bluegrass King.

Red Dawn and Bluegrass King raced into the far turn. They were still side by side. Now, the other horses started moving up on the two leaders. By the middle of the turn, there were five horses running together for the lead and heading into the stretch. The roar from the crowd was deafening. The noise was so loud that Little Red could no longer hear Andy's voice as she continued to urge him onward.

The TV announcer said, "And here they come to the top of the stretch. Red Dawn is on the rail. Bluegrass Kind and Windward are running right beside him. This has been a killing pace. How can these horses keep going at this speed?!"

The stretch of the Kentucky Futurity lay before Little Red. One quarter of a mile away was the finish line. He was now running over the spot where the race had started less than ninety seconds earlier. But to Little Red the start had seemed like years ago.

Little Red's legs felt like they were made of jelly. Even so, he flung them out and back in the easy graceful movement his mother had taught him. The blood pounded in his brain. He pushed the pain in his lungs out of his mind. He thought back to the times in the meadow with his mother. He thought, "Mother, give me strength. I cannot give up. I won't give up."

The stretch run seemed to last forever. Bluegrass King's jockey stung him with his whip. Windward's jockey used his whip, too. They wanted to get every bit of speed out of their horses that they could. But Andy did not use her whip. She urged Little Red on with a firm push on his neck with her hands. She kept saying over and over, "Let's go, boy. Keep going.

Keep going." But Little Red couldn't hear Andy. The roar of the crowd was all that he could hear.

The TV announcer said, "What a race! What a finish! Across the track and heading for the wire, it's Red Dawn, Bluegrass King, and Windward. All three are right together. It may be too close to call!"

The finish line was just ahead. Little Red's vision was blurred from the blood pounding in his head. He could not get enough air into his lungs. He felt like he was being choked. He felt like he was going to die. But, still, he knew that he had to keep going. If he were going to die from exhaustion, it would be after the finish of the Kentucky Futurity. He would not give up. He had to win.

The TV announcer said, "And here is the finish! It's Bluegrass King!! No, it's Windward.! No - it's too close to call. It is a photo finish with all three horses! I don't know who won!"

The roar of the crowd was louder than ever before. It was louder than any sound Little Red had ever heard before - or would ever hear again. It was a sound that he would never forget. It was a sound he would hear in his dreams as he grew older. It was the greatest sound he had ever heard.

The race was over. It had been the fastest Kentucky Futurity ever. People would talk about that Futurity for years to come. They would all talk about the great duel between Red Dawn and Bluegrass King and about the three-horse photo finish.

But mostly, people would talk about how a little horse from a poor little farm had run in the Kentucky Futurity. They would talk about how that small, almost unknown horse, had taken on the biggest and best three-year-old horses in the world. And they would remember how a horse with a nickname of "Little Red" had dared to race against the biggest and best, and...

he had won.

Chapter Twenty

Red Dawn went on to win many other important races. However, none of those races were quite as special to him as was his win in the Kentucky Futurity.

Andrea Bell had a chance to go to the University of Kentucky after the excitement of the Futurity. With hard work and studying between racing seasons, she was able to complete her college education. She continued her studies so that she could become a veterinarian. She became well known for being able to treat sick horses.

Every person has at least one special moment in his or her life when everything seems to be perfect. It may be a moment when they are recognized for the special things they have done. No matter what or when it is, it would become a moment etched forever in that person's memory. For Andy and Red Dawn, that one special moment was standing in the winner's circle at Miles Park after the Futurity win. In their mind's picture, Little Red was standing proudly, draped with a beautiful blanket of red roses, with Andy sitting happily on his back.

That was the very same picture that hung over the mantle in the big, beautiful new home at Richland Stables. The farm changed in many ways after the Futurity. Bright, warm, new horse barns were built. Andy went to the yearling sales each year and each year she bought horses that no one else seemed to want. She took those horses back to the big meadow at the farm and turned each one of them into winners.

Andy became famous as a person with a special gift. It seemed as though she could look at a horse and know all about it. She seemed to know what the horses were thinking and how they felt. For the rest of Andy's life, there was always an empty stall available for any unwanted horse.

Little Red was retired from racing to spend his time at Richland Stables. Once again, he and his mother roamed the big meadow and drank from the cool brook.

The old wooden barn, where it all began so many years before, was finally blown down by a big wind one night. Andy decided not to have the barn replaced with another barn. To Andy, the spot was very special. It was the place where everything good had started. Andy had a short wall built around the spot using stones from the nearby creek.

When Misty Dawn died of old age, she was buried inside the spot surrounded by the little stone wall. She had returned to rest on the very place where she had watched her young foal fight for his life many years before. She was back to where it had all started.

Richland Stables continued to be successful in racing and breeding under Andy's leadership. Little Red continued to enjoy a happy retirement in the big meadow.

Finally, the day came when Red Dawn felt very, very tired. His legs felt tired and his mind felt tired. In fact, his whole body felt tired. Little Red decided that he would lay down on the soft hay in his stall. He thought that would make him feel so much better. He closed his eyes to take a nap. Maybe he would feel stronger after the nap.

During the nap, Little Red dreamed of his past. He dreamed of the Kentucky Futurity and the great sound of the crowd cheering his win. He dreamed of standing proudly in the winner's circle with Andy on his back. He dreamed of running free in the meadow with his mother.

After the nap, he tried to stand up again, but his legs would not move. He tried again to get up, but still he was unable to stand. He decided that he would rest some more and then try again. He would not give up. He was going to stand up.

Little Red closed his eyes again. He saw his mother standing over him. She said to him, "My son you have raced long and hard. You never quit. I was always so proud of how you would never give up. Even when you lost, you always kept trying to do your best. But the race is finally over for you. You can stop running now. You can rest. You can be with me again."

The little horse lovingly called Little Red fell into a deep sleep. Sometime during that night, his big heart stopped beating. His last race was done.

Andy had Little Red buried inside the piece of ground surrounded by the little wall. He was buried beside his mother, Misty Dawn. They were together again, on the place where it had all begun so many years before.

Richland Stables and Little Red's sons and daughters continued to race and to win. Everyone agreed, however, that there would never be another horse like Little Red. He had been very special. Even his sons and daughters were not as special as he had been. He had been special because he had one thing that few other horses had or could have. He had a Big Heart.

 **Author Michael Slaughter** began his career as a Fifth-grade schoolteacher in Jefferson County Kentucky. As an elementary school teacher, he developed an Individualized Reading Program for his students. He also read a chapter from a suitable book to the class each day before the lunch period. He read to his own children each night at bedtime.

He knew what life was like on a small family farm and had always been interested in Thoroughbred Racing. This book is specifically intended for reading by 8 to 14 year olds or to be read to a class or a child at bedtime.

 **Theresa Mangis Sink** is an accomplished and an award winning artist. At one time she was a student in Michael Slaughter's elementary school class. She has been interested in painting for most of her life, having been inspired by her mother's fine art. She was also encouraged and supported in her art by her mother in law. She is a keen observer of nature and the world around her. This is her first published work and she foresees many more such projects in the future.

CPSIA information can be obtained
at www.ICGtesting.com
Printed in the USA
FSHW010136150120
65894FS